Little Sid

The Tiny Prince Who Became Buddha

Written by

Ian Lendler

Illustrated by

Xanthe Bouma

:01

First Second

New York

This is Sid.

Sid was a normal kid like you and me. Except for one thing . . .

His father was a king.
So Sid was a little lord.

Do I have to wear this? It's a bit itchy.

The life of a little lord is good.

Very, very good.

Happy birthday, little lord!

But it's also busy.

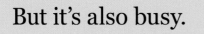

Eat fast! You have one
thousand presents
to open!

I want
to wait for my
parents.

Very, very busy.

They couldn't
make it. They had to
be somewhere else.

Oh . . .

From the moment he was born, the king and queen gave Sid anything that made him happy. He was surrounded by fun every moment of the day. From the moment he woke up . . .

To the moment he went to bed.

There was just one problem.

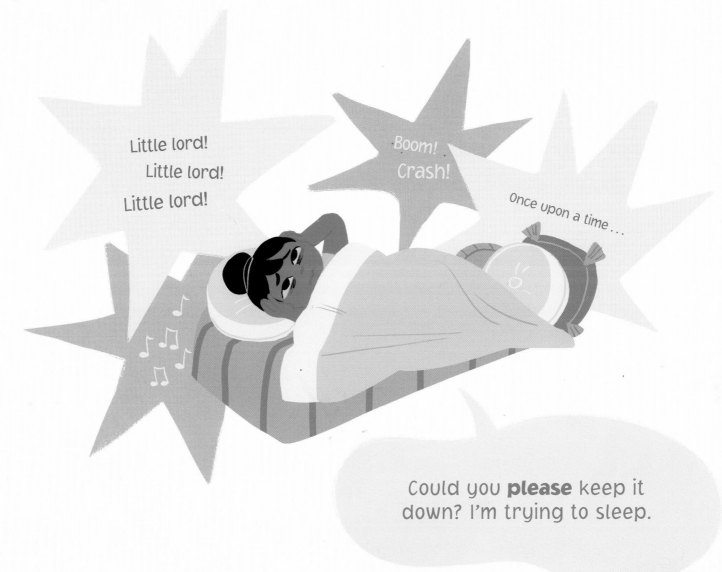

Little Sid wasn't happy.

He tried to talk about it with his parents during breakfast.

But they were always busy.
And they always said the same thing.

Sid decided he couldn't find happiness in the castle.
But maybe he could find it somewhere else.

So he left the castle.
He went to look for Happiness.

Out in the world, Little Sid walked to the nearest village.

He walked from house to house.

So Little Sid kept walking.

Happiness was going to be harder to find than he thought.

He walked up the Mountain of the Three Wise Ones.
He soon came to a stream where a sleepy-looking man was fishing.

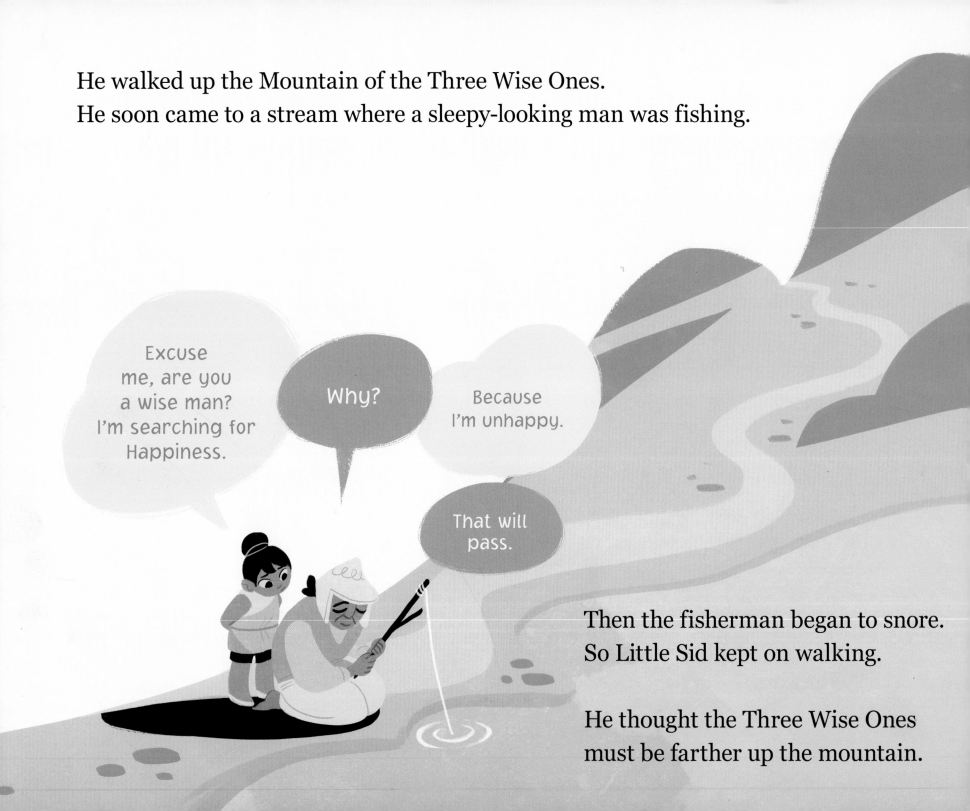

Excuse me, are you a wise man? I'm searching for Happiness.

Why?

Because I'm unhappy.

That will pass.

Then the fisherman began to snore.
So Little Sid kept on walking.

He thought the Three Wise Ones must be farther up the mountain.

Up and up he walked until a mighty river blocked his path.
On the other side, he saw a woman in a tree.

Excuse me, are you a wise woman? I'm searching for Happiness. How do I get to the other side?

The tree-woman looked at the river. Then she said . . .

You are already on the other side.

Little Sid thought that was the dumbest thing he'd ever heard.

But he thought about it some more.

Finally, he said . . .

Suddenly, a tiger leapt out of the forest and charged at Little Sid.

So Little Sid ran.
He ran and ran . . .

until he ran off a cliff!

AAAAAGH!

Fortunately, he grabbed
a vine and hung on.

Whew!

Unfortunately, a mouse appeared
and began to nibble the vine.

Stop that!
Shoo, mouse,
shoo!

But the mouse wouldn't shoo.
The vine was about to break.
Little Sid was going to die!

I hate this
mountain.

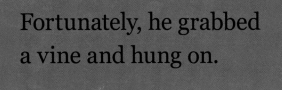

That's when he noticed a strawberry
growing on the vine. Since this might be
the last meal of his life, he took a bite.

Then the mouse spoke.
It said, "How does it taste?"

Without thinking, Little Sid said . . .

"Delicious."

A fishing line appeared in front of Sid.
He grabbed the hook and it pulled him up to safety.

When Sid walked down off the mountain,
something about him seemed . . . different.

He thought different.

He acted different.

He *was* different.

That evening at dinner, Little Sid decided to make some changes.

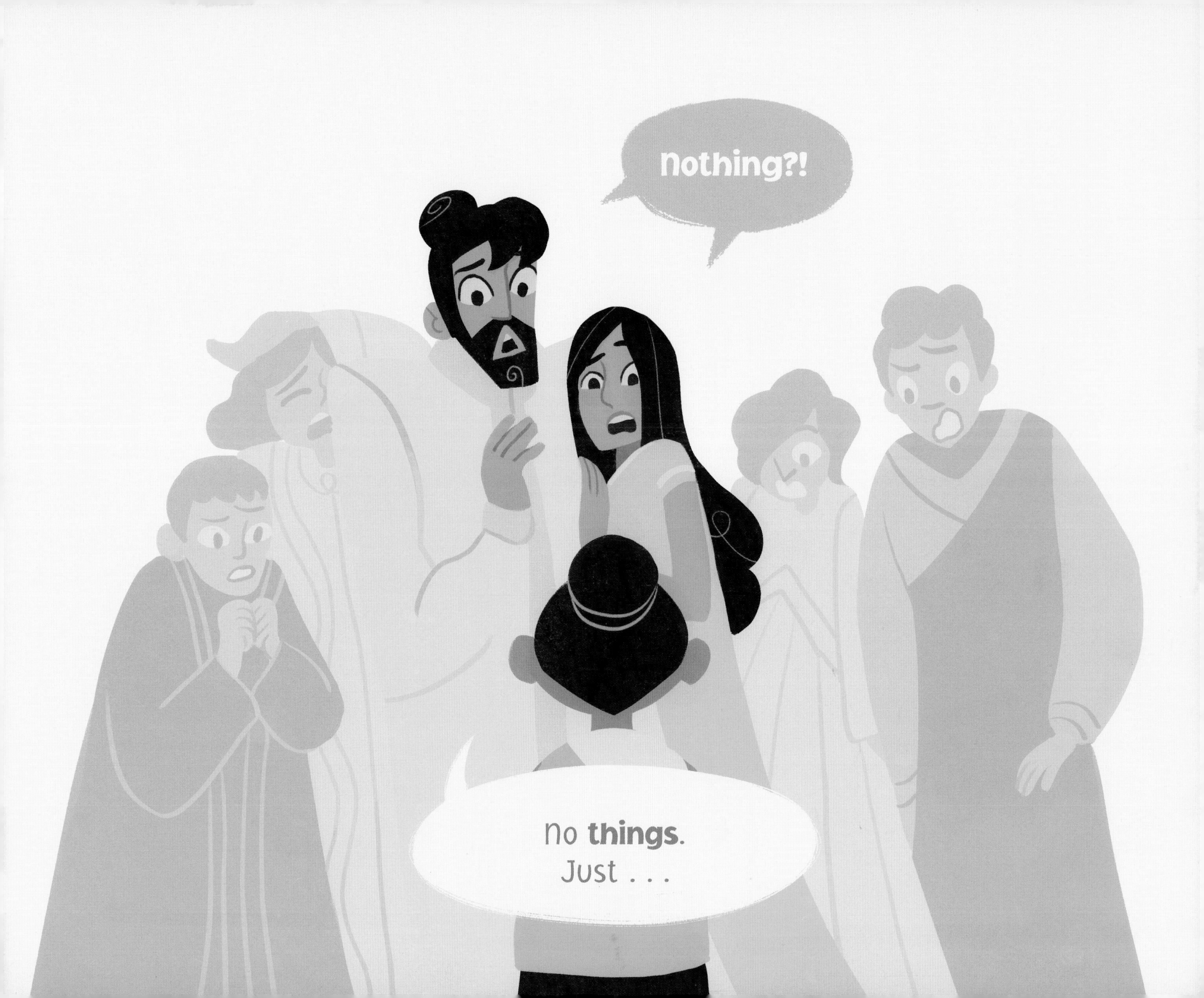
Nothing?!
No **things**. Just . . .

Siddhārtha Gautama aka the Buddha

Little Sid is a real historical figure. His full name was Siddhārtha Gautama and he lived sometime between the 6th and 4th centuries BC. He was born a prince in what is now the country of Nepal.

Despite being raised in luxury, he was unhappy with the idea of suffering in the world. He abandoned his wealth and royal title to become a penniless wandering monk.

While meditating one day, Siddhārtha is said to have achieved "enlightenment." He believed that anyone who practices kind thoughts, kind deeds, and meditation can free themselves from suffering. From this moment on, he became known as "the Buddha," meaning "he who is awake."

Siddhārtha spent the rest of his life spreading his message. Breaking from tradition, he taught both men and women and people of every race and class. The popularity of his philosophy quickly grew, and today there are almost 500 million Buddhists, making it the fourth most popular religion in the world.

:01
First Second

Text copyright © 2018 by Ian Lendler
Illustrations copyright © 2018 by Xanthe Bouma

Published by First Second
First Second is an imprint of Roaring Brook Press, a division of Holtzbrinck Publishing Holdings Limited Partnership
175 Fifth Avenue, New York, NY 10010

Library of Congress Control Number:
2017940049

ISBN: 978-1-62672-636-9

Our books may be purchased in bulk for promotional, educational, or business use. Please contact your local bookseller or the Macmillan Corporate and Premium Sales Department at (800) 221-7945 ext. 5442 or by e-mail at MacmillanSpecialMarkets@macmillan.com.

First edition 2018

Book design by Andrew Arnold
Printed in China by RR Donnelley Asia Printing Solutions Ltd., Dongguan City, Guangdong Province

1 3 5 7 9 10 8 6 4 2

Drawn digitally and colored in Adobe Photoshop using Kyle T. Webster's gouache brush set on a Wacom Cintiq.